W9-CAJ-193

UNO, DOS, TRES: ONE, TWO, THREE

by PAT MORA
Illustrated by BARBARA LAVALLEE

CLARION BOOKS/New York

Clarion Books
a Houghton Mifflin Company imprint
215 Park Avenue South, New York, NY 10003
Text copyright © 1996 by Pat Mora
Illustrations copyright © 1996 by Barbara Lavallee

The illustrations for this book were executed in watercolors on 300-lb. Fabriano watercolor board.
The text was set in 22/25-point Goudy.

All rights reserved.

For information about permission to reproduce selections from this book,
write to Permissions, Houghton Mifflin Company,
215 Park Avenue South, New York, NY 10003.

For information about this and other Houghton Mifflin trade and reference books and multimedia products,
visit The Bookstore at Houghton Mifflin on the World Wide Web at (http://www.hmco.com/trade/).

Printed in the USA.

Library of Congress Cataloging-in-Publication Data

Mora, Pat.
Uno, dos, tres : One, two, three / by Pat Mora ; illustrated by Barbara Lavallee.
p.   cm.
Summary: Pictures depict two sisters going from shop to shop buying birthday presents for their mother.
Rhyming text presents numbers from one to ten in English and Spanish.
ISBN 0-395-67294-5
[1. Birthdays—Fiction.   2. Counting.   3. Stories in rhyme.   4. Spanish language materials.]
I. Lavallee, Barbara, ill.   II. Title.   III. Title: One, two, three.
PZ8.3.M794Un   1996
[E]—dc20   94-15337
CIP
AC

HOR   10   9   8   7   6   5   4   3   2   1

For my daughters, Libby and Cissy,
who give me so many wonderful surprises
—P.M.

To Marilyn—
with peaches, prunes, and happy times
—B.L.

uno   one

We'll buy Mamá a sun.

dos   two

Two doves that say coo-coo.

11

tres   three

Bells ring-ringing in our tree.

13

14   uno   dos   tres

one   two   three

cuatro four

Piñatas at the door.

cinco   five

Puppets dance as if alive.

seis   six

Castanet click-clicks.

uno   dos   tres

four   five   six

uno   dos   tres
cuatro   cinco   seis

one two three
four five six

siete   seven

Stars twink-twinkling in heaven.

ocho   eight

Small baskets, pots, and plates.

nueve   nine

Wood animals are fine.

diez   ten

A band of marching men.

36   uno   dos   tres   one   two   three

cuatro   cinco   seis   four   five   six

uno   dos   tres
cuatro cinco   seis

one two three
four five six

39

uno dos tres cuatro cinco
seis siete ocho nueve diez

one   two   three   four   five
six   seven   eight   nine   ten

¡Feliz cumpleaños, Mamá!

42

Happy birthday, Mama!

Author's Note

Since I grew up on the border, I started enjoying Mexican markets when I was a little girl. I've always liked the life in the markets—the music, the voices of the vendors, the splashes of color, the varied textures of the wares, the humor and inventiveness of folk artists, the sounds of Spanish and English weaving through the air.

Markets are wonderful places to buy surprises for those we love of all ages. We count our gifts in English, in Spanish—one, two, three . . . uno, dos, tres—enjoying the pleasure of being bilingual.

Pronunciation Guide

uno (OO-noh): one
dos (dohs): two
tres (trehs): three
cuatro (KWAH-troh): four
cinco (SEEN-koh): five
seis (SEH-ees): six
siete (SEE-eh-teh): seven
ocho (OH-choh): eight
nueve (NWEH-beh): nine
diez (dee-EHS): ten
Mamá (mah-MAH): Mama
piñata (pee-NYAH-tah): piñata
¡Feliz cumpleaños! (feh-LEES koom-pleh-AH-nyohs): Happy birthday!